Art Therapy

OVER 100 IMAGES TO INSPIRE CREATIVITY AND RELAXATION

EGMONT
We bring stories to life

First published by Hachette Livre in 2015
Published in Great Britain 2016
by Egmont UK Limited, The Yellow Building,
1 Nicholas Road, London W11 4AN

Direction: Catherine Saunier-Talec
Art Director: Antoine Béon
Project Manager: Anne Vallet
Design and Realisation: Nicolas Beaujouan
Cover Illustrations and pages 11, 45, 55, 69, 97: Kanthesis
Production: Amélie Latsch

ISBN 978 1 4052 7991 8
62216/2
Printed in Spain

For more great *Star Wars* books, visit www.egmont.co.uk/starwars

Colouring taps into the psyche of those who practise it. It stands to reason then that even the Masters of the Jedi Order must have devoted themselves to the holy practice, from the leaders of the temple on Coruscant to those residing in the depths of the muddy backwaters on Dagobah.

In our part of the galaxy, nearer our time, the psychologist and psychiatrist Carl Gustav Jung, deeply depressed for some thirteen years, recorded his dreams and his anxieties as tales and colourings in what is now considered to be an essential work of modern psychology, *The Red Book*. By colouring mandalas and monsters, and by using colour to capture his anxieties and his dreams, Jung was reinterpreting his vast knowledge of human mythology in order to rediscover the way of reaching tranquillity, of attaining an essential mental balance.

Incidentally, this is where Jung and *Star Wars* meet again: both have in their own ways blended heroic tales and mythology to offer hope and to define a way to produce something that enables us to find ourselves. What could be more obvious than to offer this "therapeutic" colouring based on the most famous contemporary pop mythology of them all?

So relax, turn the page, and, to paraphrase Yoda: "May the *colouring* force be with you."

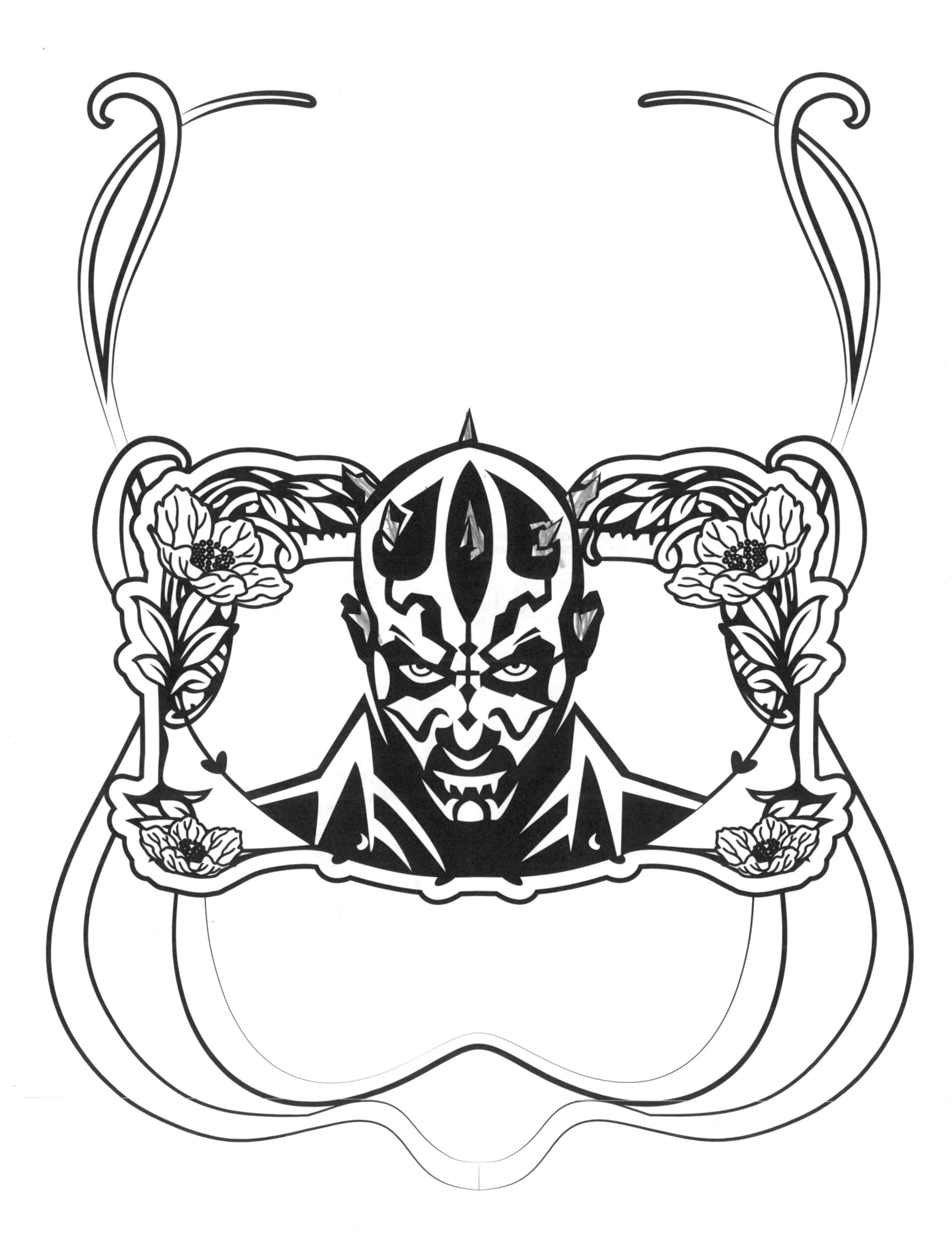

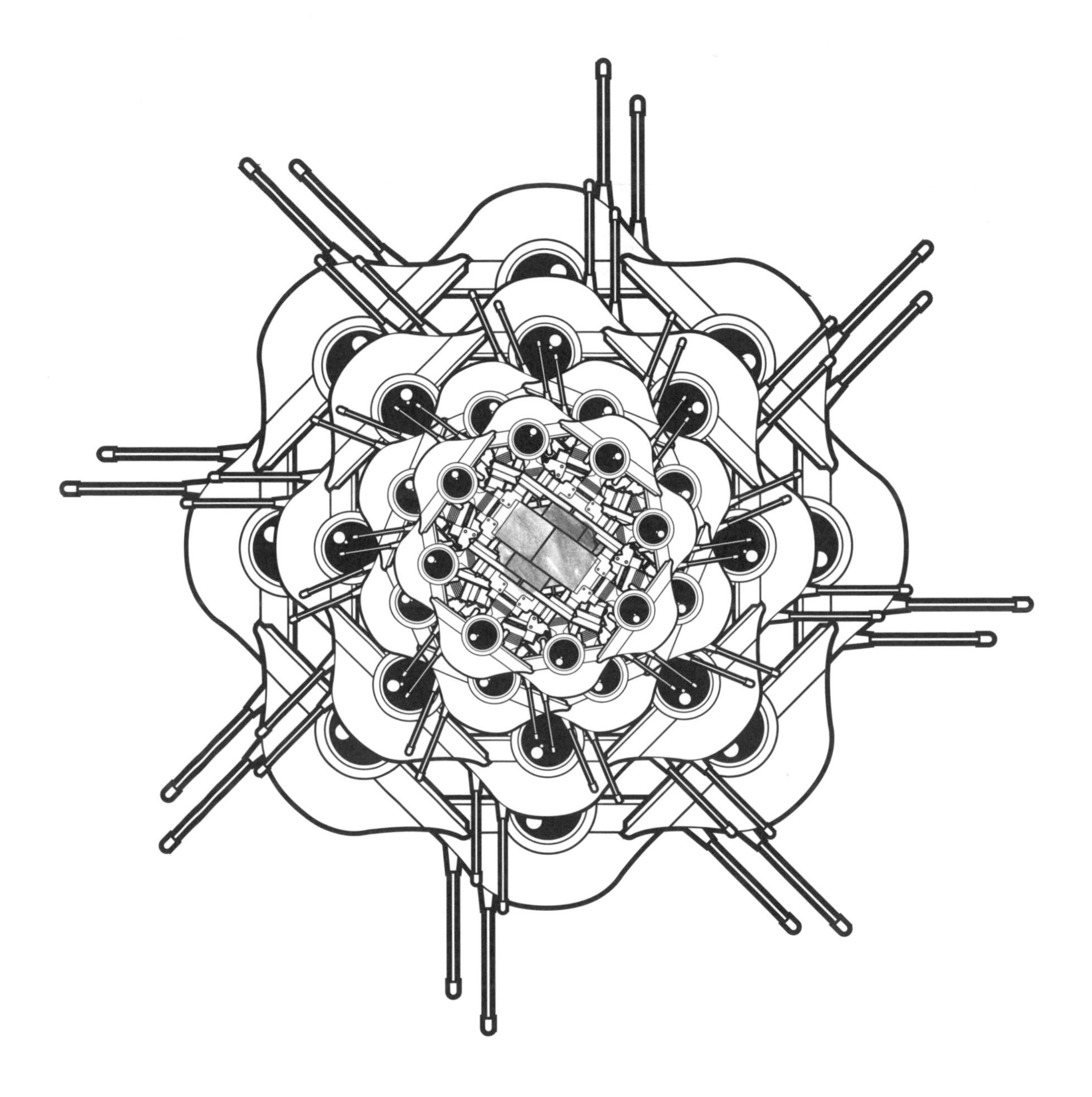

KASHYYYK

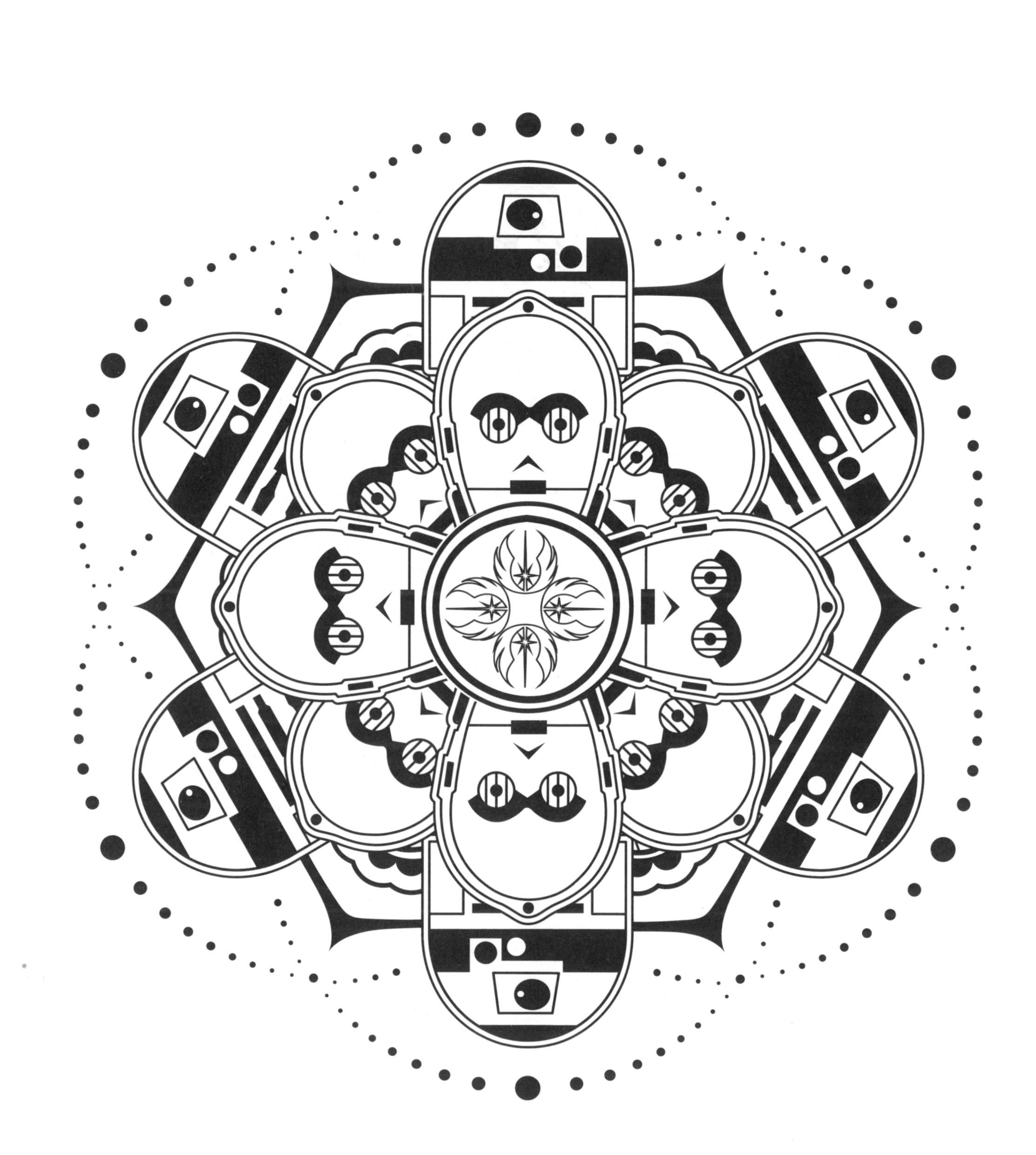

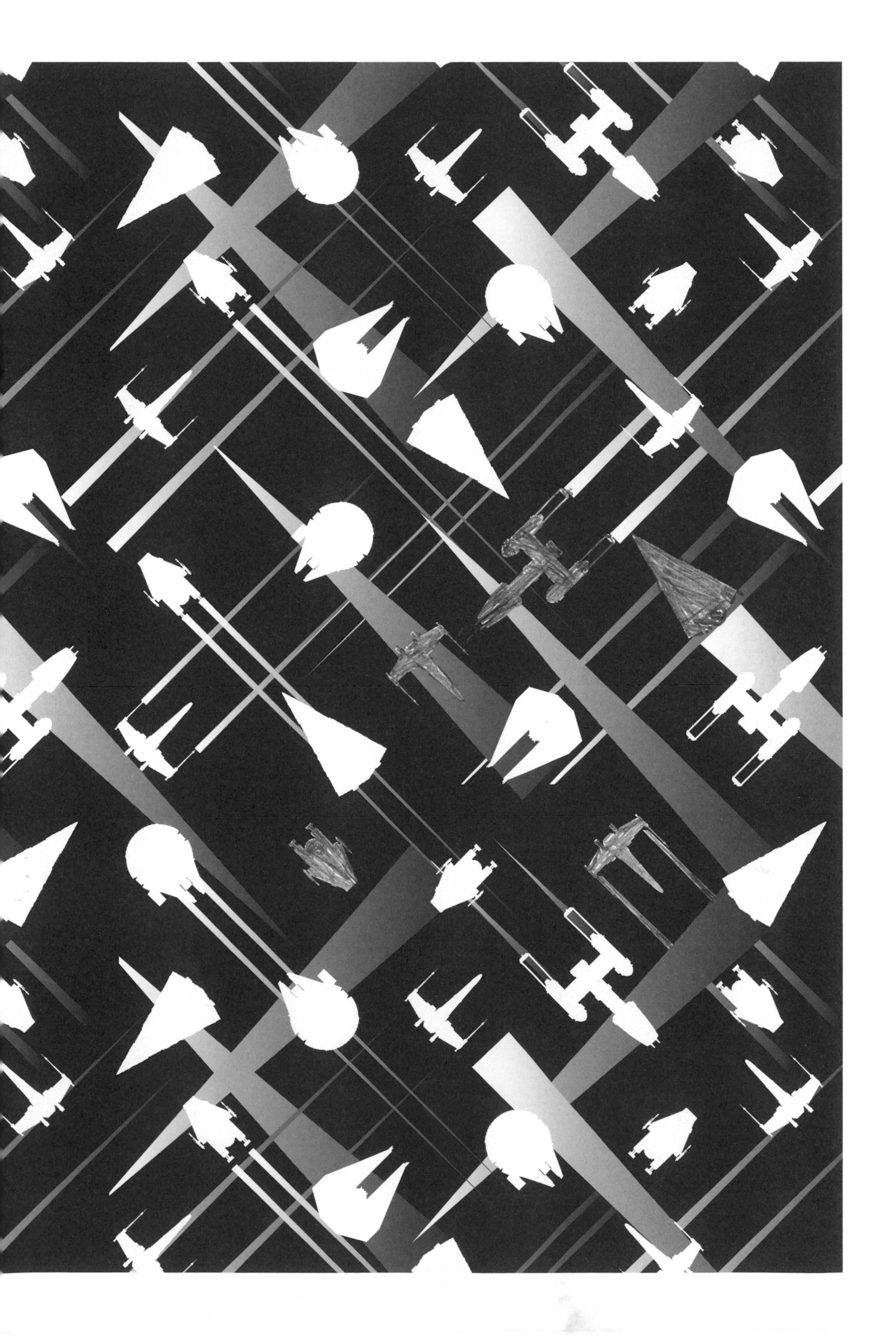

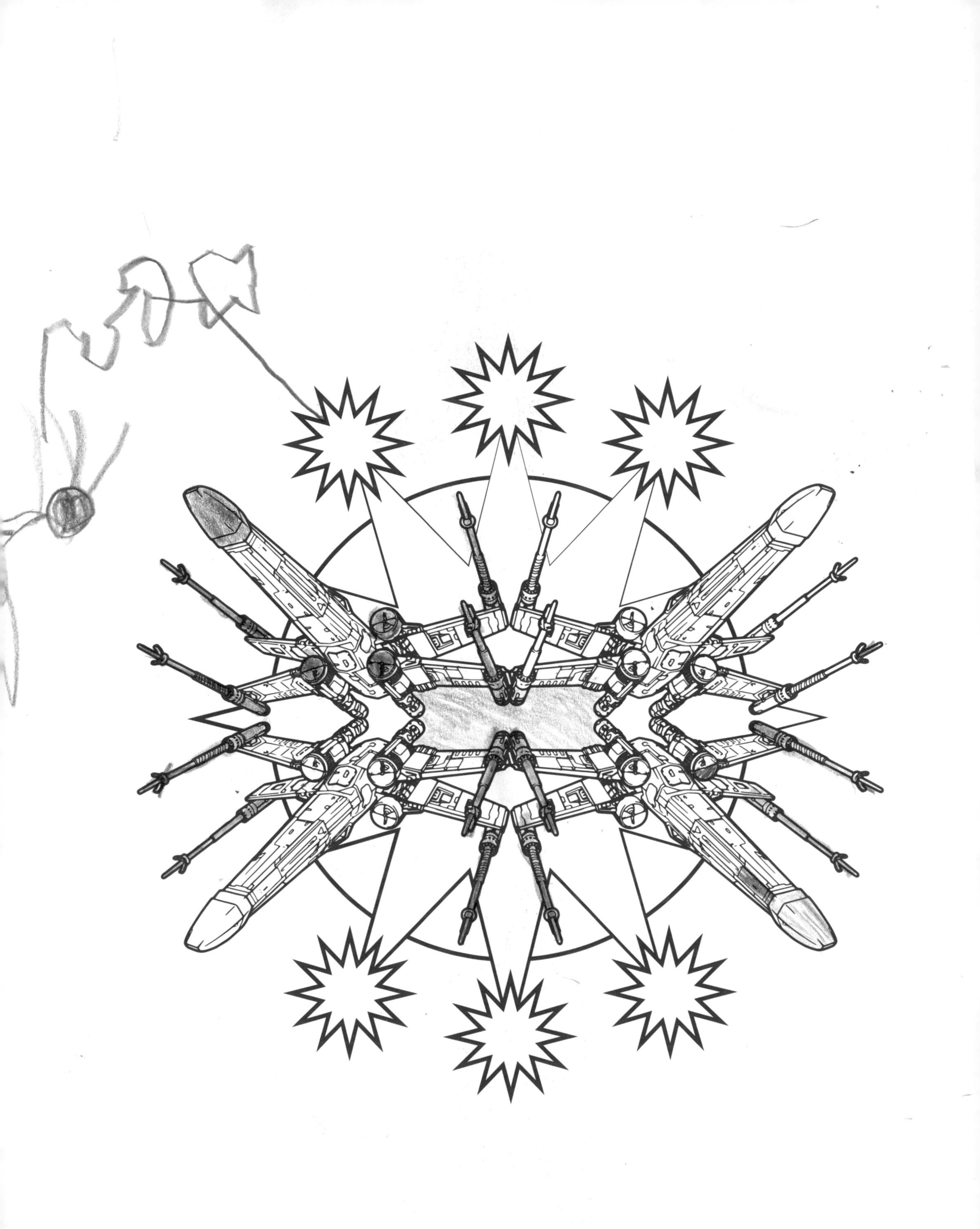

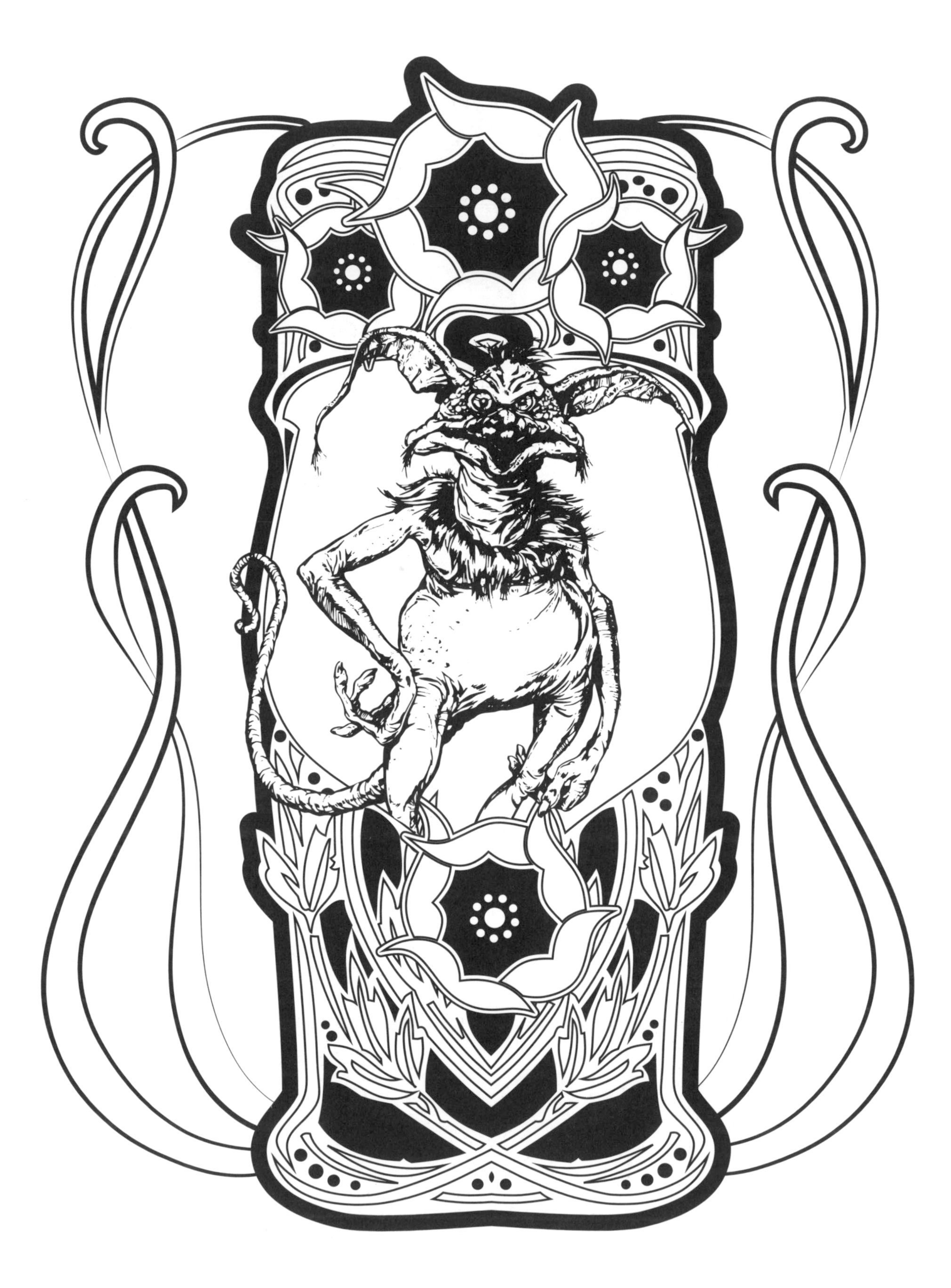

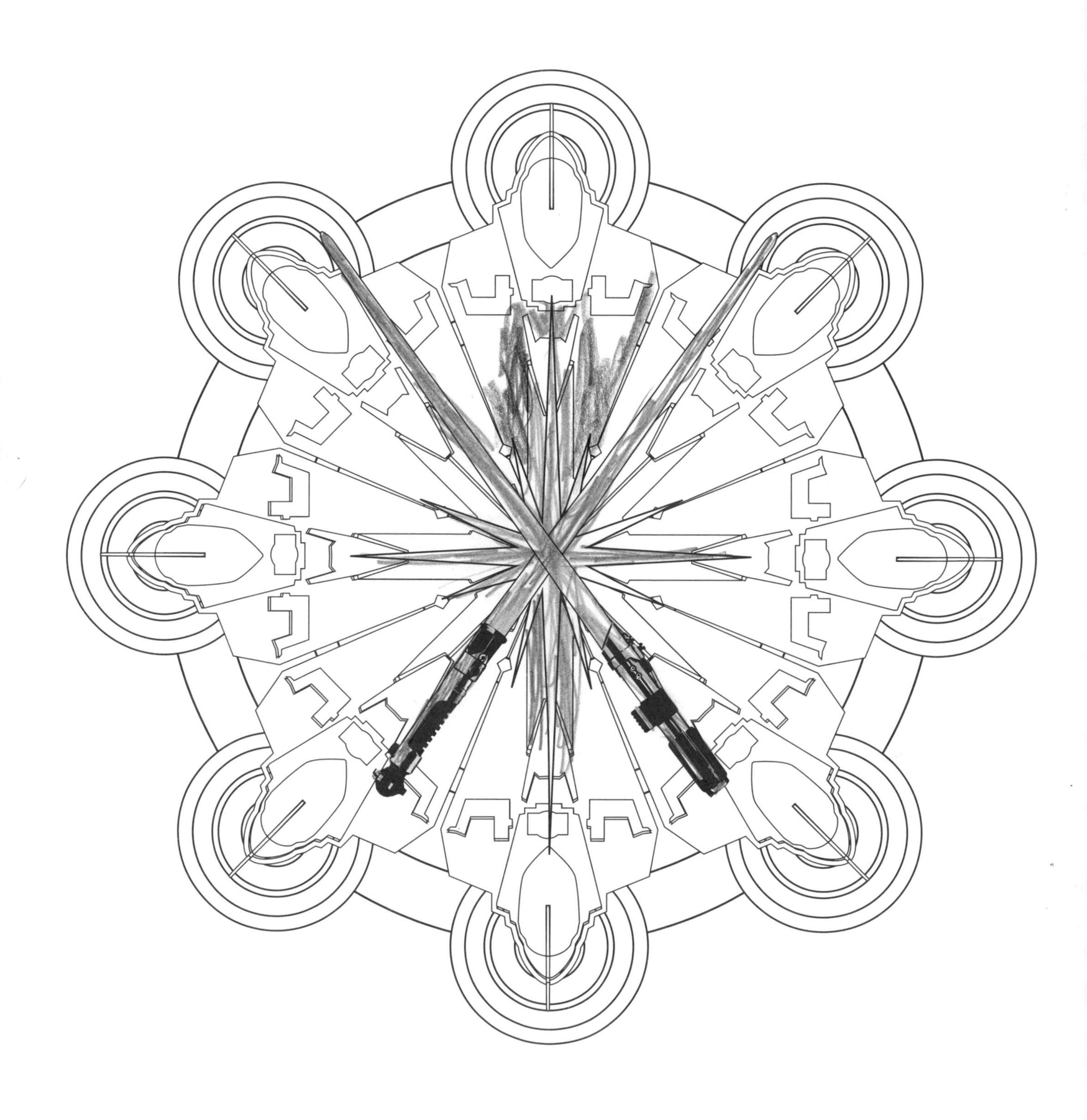

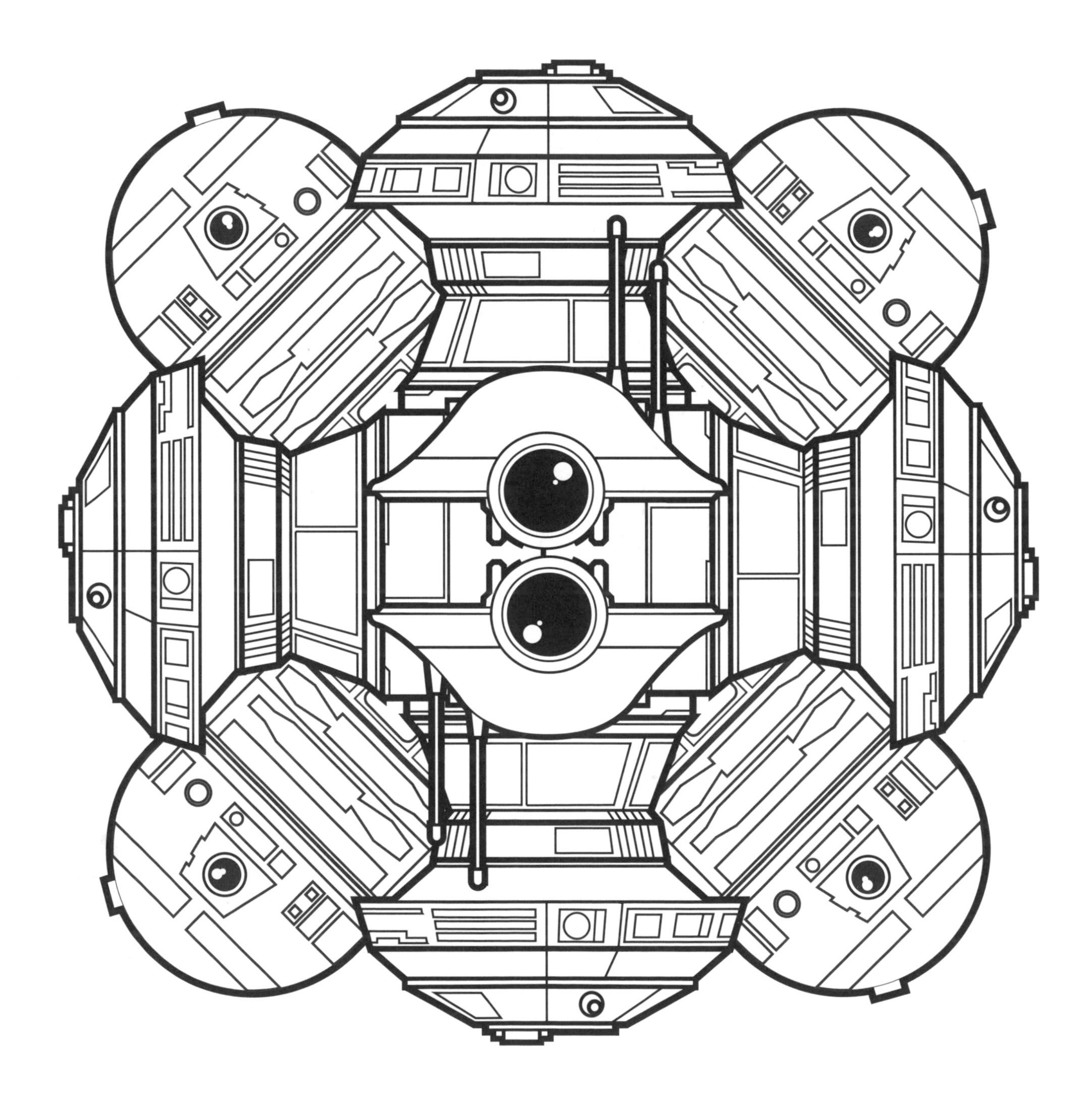

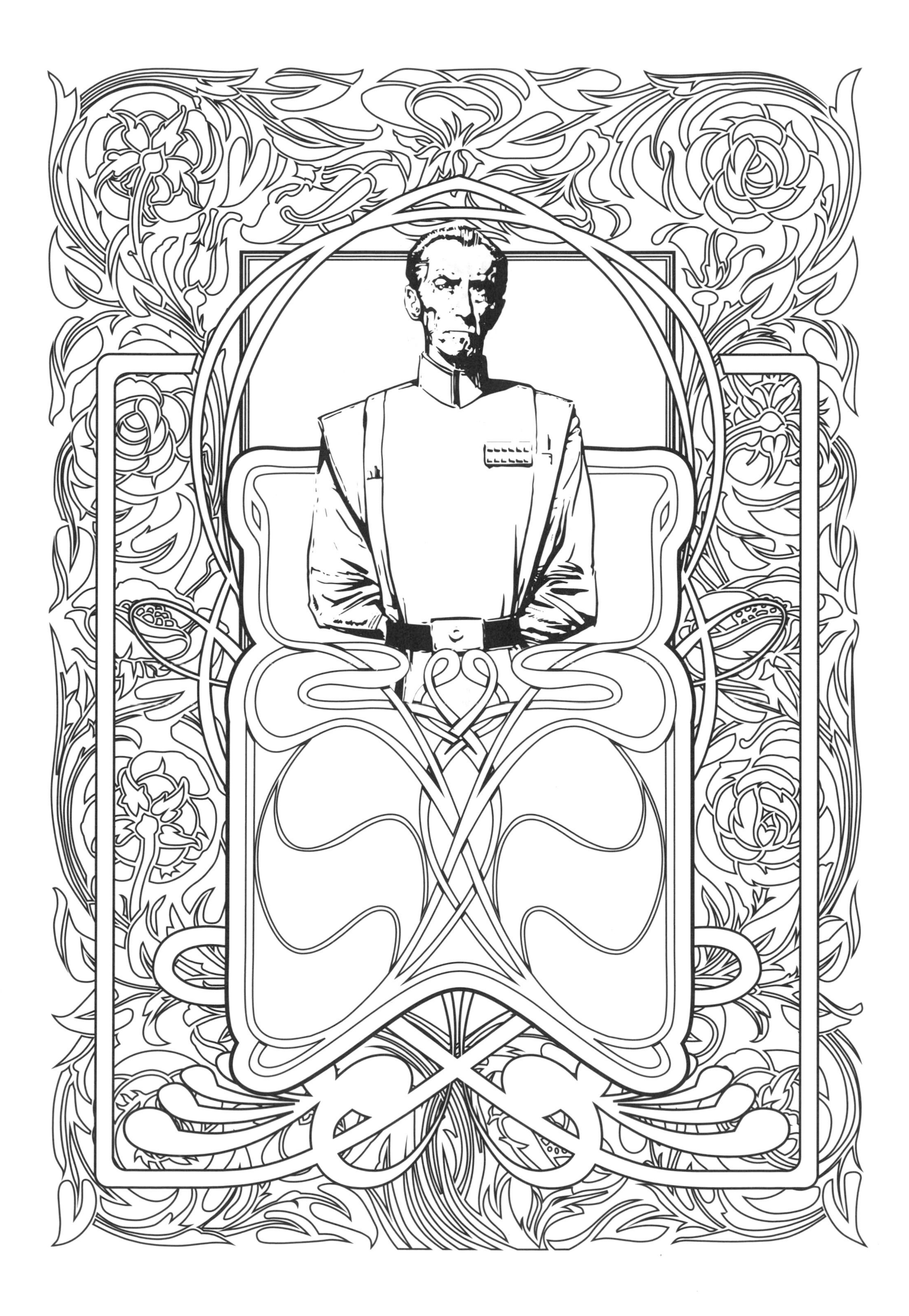

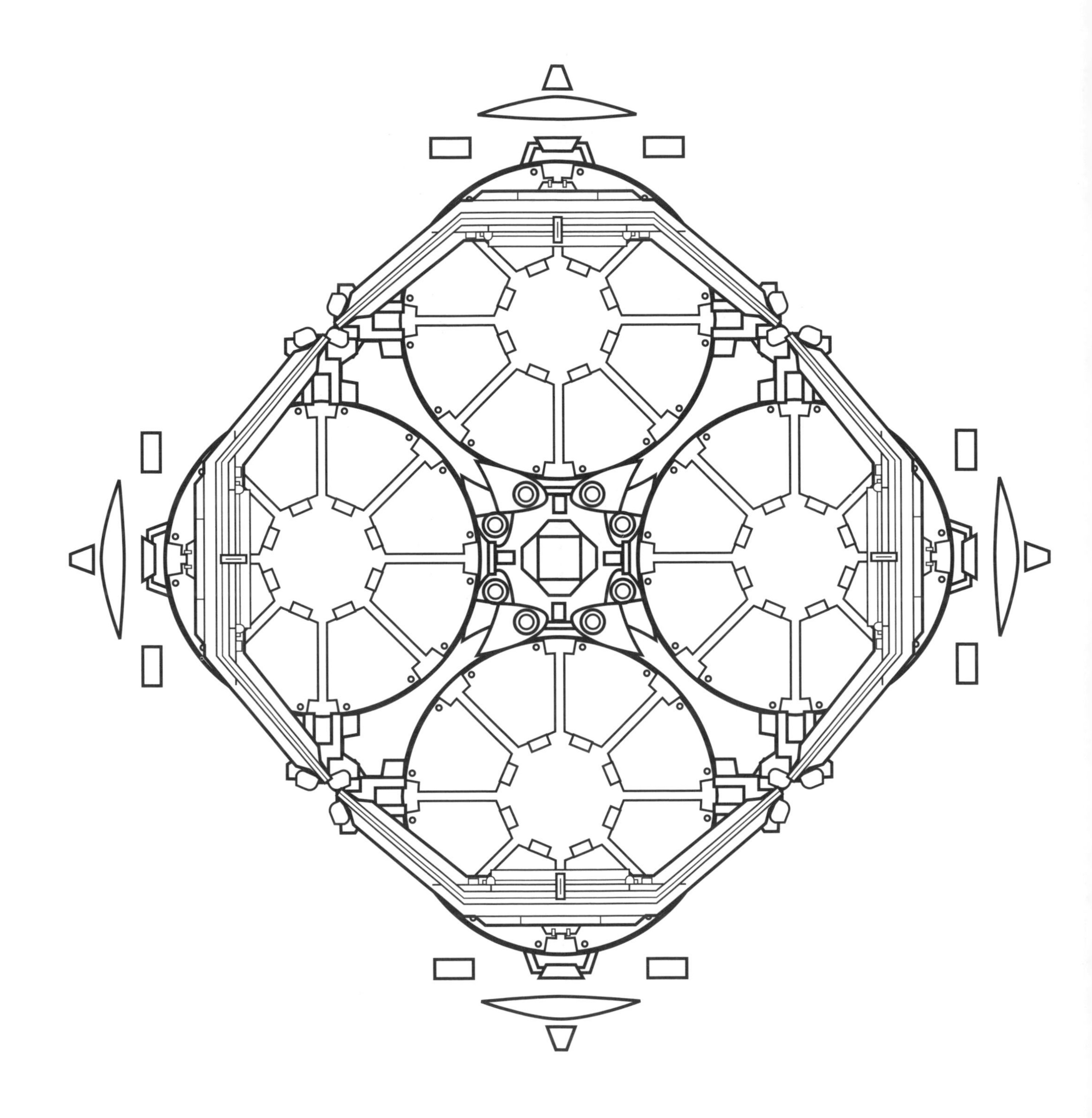

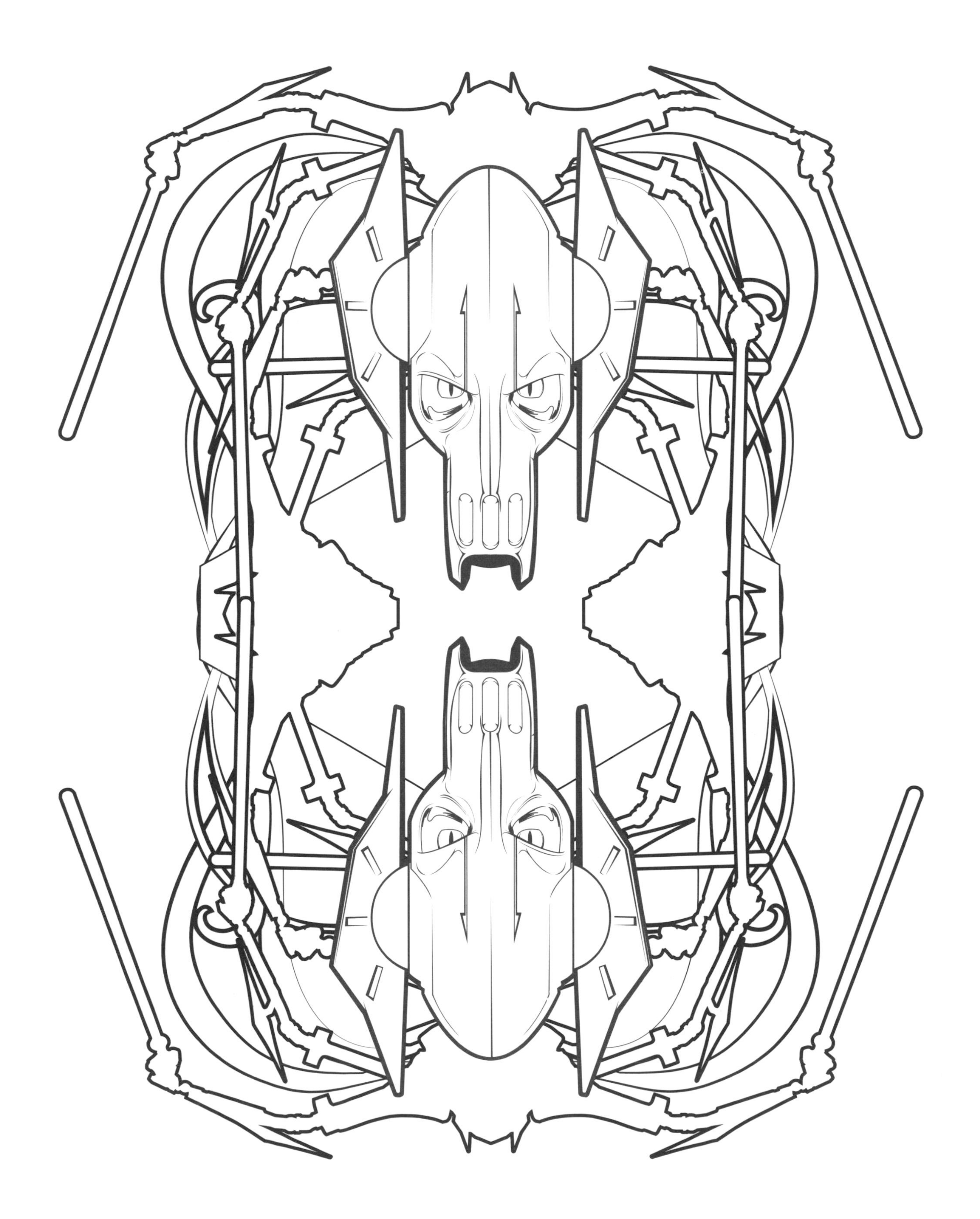

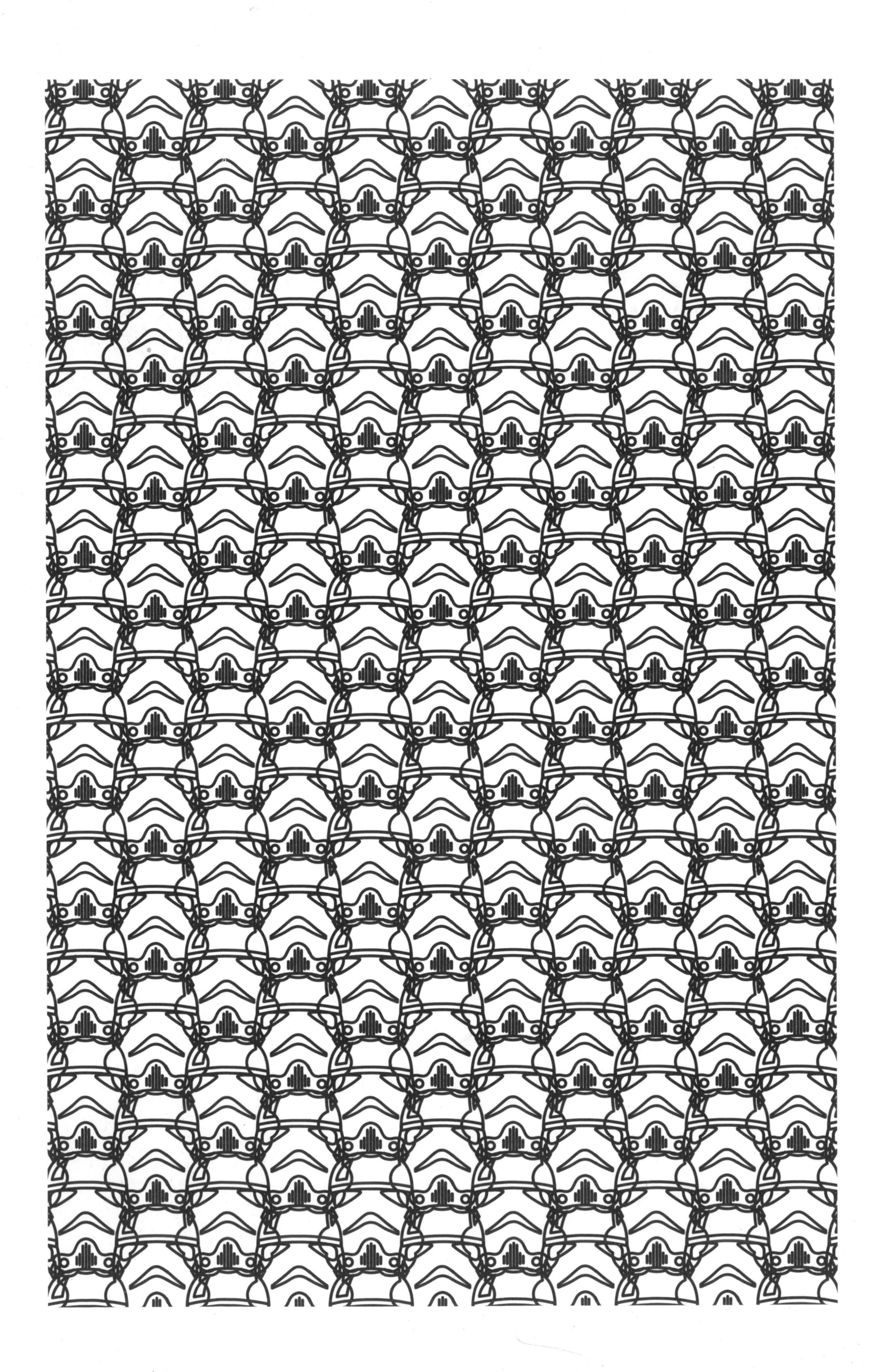